iCarly™ iDon't Wanna Fight!

Adapted by Leigh Olsen

SCHOLASTIC INC.

New York   Toronto   London   Auckland

Sydney   Mexico City   New Delhi   Hong Kong

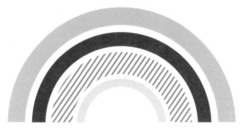

ISBN: 978-0-545-20127-8

Published by Scholastic Inc.
SCHOLASTIC and associated logos are trademarks and/or registered trademarks of Scholastic Inc.

12 11 10 9 8 7 6 5 4 3   10 11 12 13 14 15/0

Designed by Angela Jun
Printed in the U.S.A.   40
First printing, January 2010

Carly, Sam, and Freddie were at Carly's loft. They were watching videos sent in by viewers. They needed to pick some for their Web show, *iCarly*.

The next video was from two guys named Chris.

"We're best friends," said one Chris.

"And we're the world's greatest meat drummers!" said the other Chris.

The two boys stepped behind a table. It was covered with different kinds of meat. Then they used their hands to drum on the meat. It made lots of gross noises. Carly, Sam, and Freddie loved it.

"I give them a ten!" said Carly.

"Let's put the best friends' video on *iCarly*!" Freddie added.

"Hey, Sam," said Carly. "Speaking of best friends, do you know what today is?"

"Is it the twenty-fifth?" asked Sam.

"Yep!" said Carly.

"What's the twenty-fifth?" asked Freddie.

"It's our anniversary. Sam and I met five years ago," Carly answered.

Sam got a dreamy look on her face. "I remember it like it was only five years ago . . ."

Sam and Carly met in third grade. It had been lunchtime. Carly was eating a tuna sandwich when Sam walked up.

"Can I have your sandwich?" Sam asked Carly.

"No way!" said Carly.

Sam pushed Carly out of her seat. Then she stole Carly's sandwich.

But Carly wasn't going to let Sam bully her around. So she got up and pushed Sam. Then Carly took back her tuna sandwich.

"Hey, you're pretty cool!" said Sam. They had been friends ever since.

"I can't believe we became friends over a tuna sandwich," Sam said.

"I know," said Carly. "I got you something for our friendship anniversary."

Sam looked surprised. "You got me a present?"

Carly gave Sam a little wrapped box. Sam ripped it open.

Sam couldn't believe her eyes. "You made me an *iCarly* T-shirt!"

"It's no big deal," said Carly. But it was a big deal to Carly. She had worked very hard on the T-shirt. And she was very excited that Sam liked it.

"I'm gonna get *you* something awesome too," Sam said. "Like tickets to the Cuddle Fish concert on Friday!"

"I would love to go. But that concert is sold out," said Carly.

"I'll figure it out," Sam promised.

The next day, Sam had an idea. There was a boy at school named Rodney. Rodney was always selling stuff to kids at school. Sam knew Rodney would have Cuddle Fish tickets. Sam found Rodney at his locker.

"I need tickets to the Cuddle Fish concert," Sam told Rodney.

"I'll trade you your *iCarly* shirt for the tickets," Rodney said.

Sam wasn't sure what to do. Should she trade the shirt Carly gave her for the tickets?

Sam was late for rehearsal that afternoon. Carly and Freddie were waiting for her.

"Where *is* she?" asked Carly.

Finally, Sam burst in. She was wearing Rodney's shirt.

"Where were you? And why are you wearing that?" asked Carly.

"I'm wearing this ugly shirt because I got us tickets to the Cuddle Fish concert!" said Sam.

"Wow! Where did you get these?" said Carly. She was so excited.

"From Rodney," said Sam. "I traded him the *iCarly* shirt for the tickets!"

Carly frowned.

"You traded the shirt I made you?" she asked.

"I traded it for something you really wanted," said Sam.

Carly was very angry.

"That was the first *iCarly* T-shirt ever!" yelled Carly. "I spent two weeks making it for you!"

"You said it was no big deal!" said Sam.

"Of course it was a big deal!" said Carly.

"Guys," said Freddie. "It's time to film *iCarly*!"

Carly and Sam followed Freddie into the elevator. They fought the whole way up to the studio.

Freddie counted down to showtime. But Carly and Sam were still arguing.

Then the show went on air. Carly and Sam quit fighting. They smiled and greeted their fans. Then they showed a video from a viewer.

"Check out this clip of a little girl giving her mom a surprise birthday gift," said Sam.

On the screen, a mom untied the bow of a huge present. Her daughter jumped out of the box. The girl was holding a rubber chicken. The mom screamed.

"What a birthday present!" said Sam.

"Yes," said Carly. "I'm sure that little girl's mom would never trade that present."

"What if she traded it for something they could do together? Then her daughter would be happy," said Sam.

"Maybe you should do the show *without* me!" yelled Carly.

"*You* do it without *me*!" said Sam.

Freddie didn't want the *iCarly* fans to see them fighting. He turned the camera off.

Carly and Sam were still not getting along a few days later. They were at school when Rodney walked by. He was wearing the *iCarly* shirt.

"Hey, Sam," said Rodney. "I love my shirt."

Carly gave Sam a dirty look. Sam rolled her eyes.

Freddie came over to them. "Please stop fighting," he said. "What happens to *iCarly* if you don't make up? Think of our fans. And me!"

"Maybe Freddie's right," Carly said to Sam. "We were just trying to do something nice for each other."

"I'll say I'm sorry if you will," Sam said.

Just then, a girl named Tareen ran up to Sam. "Hey, thanks for taking me to the Cuddle Fish concert!" Tareen said. Then she left for class.

Carly stared at Sam. "You went to the concert without me?" Carly was even angrier than before.

"Oh, no," said Freddie. "We were so close."

Carly and Sam had to film *iCarly* the next night. They were still arguing. But this time, Freddie had a plan.

"Tonight, we do the show my way. Or I quit," said Freddie.

"Fine," sighed Carly. "What do you want us to do?"

"Go put your hair in ponytails," said Freddie.

   The show went on air. Freddie stood
in front of the camera. Sam and Carly
were behind him. Their ponytails were tied
to ropes. And the ropes were attached to
the ceiling.
   "Hi," said Freddie. "Welcome to *iCarly*.
Tonight, the show is going to be a little
different."

"Carly and Sam are in a fight," Freddie went on. "But it is going to end tonight. You, the fans of *iCarly,* are going to decide who is right. You can vote at iCarly-dot-com after the show.

"Carly and Sam will each give their side of the story," Freddie said. "But if either girl interrupts or says something mean, I will yank on her ponytail with these ropes. The first girl to talk will be Carly."

Sam was holding the sound-effects remote control. She pressed a button that played a loud *booooo*.

"Hey!" said Carly. "She pressed the *boo* button!"

Freddie yanked one of the ropes. The rope pulled on Sam's ponytail.

"*Ow!*" said Sam.

"Carly, you may begin," said Freddie.

"I gave Sam an *iCarly* T-shirt," said Carly. "I worked so hard to make it. It was a really special gift. And she traded it for concert tickets."

"You wanted to go to that concert!" shouted Sam. But Freddie pulled the rope again. "Ow!" she said.

Carly continued. "Then Sam went to the concert without me. And she hasn't said she's sorry."

Next, it was Sam's turn to explain herself.

"Carly really wanted to go to the Cuddle Fish concert," Sam said. "So I traded the shirt to get something Carly wanted. And Carly wouldn't go to the concert with me."

"I would have gone if you said you were sorry!" shouted Carly.

"Freddie!" said Sam. "She interrupted! Yank her ponytail!"

"No, I'm going to allow it," said Freddie.

"Give me that rope!" said Sam. Sam took
Carly's rope from Freddie. She yanked down
as hard as she could.

"*Owww!*" yelled Carly.

Then Carly tugged Sam's rope.

"*Owww!*" yelled Sam.

The two girls pulled back and forth on each
other's ponytails.

"You guys! Stop pulling the ropes!"
Freddie shouted. But it was no use.

After the show, Carly, Sam, and Freddie sat in Carly's living room.

"My hair hurts," said Carly.

"Mine, too," said Sam.

"Would you please hurry up and count the votes?" Carly asked Freddie.

"Do you promise that the loser will say she's sorry?" he asked.

The girls agreed.

"Sam, the number of *iCarly* viewers who think you are right is 693. And Carly, you got 705," Freddie said.

"Ha!" Carly said to Sam.

"Not so fast!" said Freddie. "There was a third option. It said, 'Carly and Sam are both acting dumb. They should just make up and be friends again.'"

"How many people voted for that one?" asked Carly.

"253,719," said Freddie. "Our fans don't like it when best friends fight. Neither do I."

Carly and Sam both felt silly. Sam even had a tear in her eye.

"Aw, you're crying," said Carly.

"Freddie is just such a dork," Sam said. "It makes me sad sometimes."

"I'm sorry," Carly said to Sam.

"I'm sorry, too," said Sam.

The girls hugged. Carly and Sam knew that their fans were right. They were best friends. And they didn't want to fight ever again.